DEMAIN PUBLISHING

<u>Short Sharp Shocks!</u>

Book 0: Dirty Paws - Dean M. Drinkel
Book 1: Patient K - Barbie Wilde
Book 2: The Stranger & The Ribbon – Tim Dry
Book 3: Asylum Of Shadows – Stephanie Ellis
Book 4: Monster Beach – Ritchie Valentine Smith
Book 5: Beasties & Other Stories – Martin Richmond
Book 6: Every Moon Atrocious – Emile-Louis Tomas Jouvet
Book 7: A Monster Met – Liz Tuckwell
Book 8: The Intruders & Other Stories – Jason D. Brawn
Book 9: The Other – David Youngquist
Book 10: Symphony Of Blood – Leah Crowley
Book 11: Shattered – Anthony Watson
Book 12: The Devil's Portion – Benedict J. Jones
Book 13: Cinders Of A Blind Man Who Could See – Kev Harrison
Book 14: Dulce Et Decorum Est – Dan Howarth
Book 15: Blood, Bears & Dolls – Allison Weir
Book 16: The Forest Is Hungry – Chris Stanley
Book 17: The Town That Feared Dusk – Calvin Demmer
Book 18: Night Of The Rider – Alyson Faye
Book 19: Isidora's Pawn – Erik Hofstatter
Book 20: Plain – D.T. Griffith
Book 21: Supermassive Black Mass – Matthew Davis

The Fallen – Anthony Watson
The Underclass – Dan Weatherer
Cheslyn Myre – Dan Weatherer
Greenbeard – John Travis
Tower Of Raven – Kevin M. Folliard
Welcome Home Natalie – Reyna Young
Little Bird – TR Hitchman
Society Place – Andrew David Barker
Axe – Terry Grimwood

The 'A QUIET APOCALYPSE' Series

A Quiet Apocalypse – Dave Jeffery
Cathedral (A Quiet Apocalypse Book 2) – Dave Jeffery
The Samaritan (A Quiet Apocalypse Book 3) – Dave Jeffery
A Silent Dystopia – Edited by D.T. Griffith

General Fiction

Joe – Terry Grimwood
Finding Jericho – Dave Jeffery

Science Fiction Collections

Vistas – Chris Kelso

Horror Fiction Collections

Distant Frequencies – Frank Duffy
Where We Live – Tim Cooke
Night Voices – Paul Edwards & Frank Duffy

Book 46: The Birthday Girl & Other Stories –
	Christopher Beck
Book 47: Crowded House & Other Stories - S.J.
	Budd
Book 48: Hand To Mouth – Deborah Sheldon
Book 49: Moonlight Gunshot Mallet Flame / A
	Little Death – Alicia Hilton
Book 50: Dark Corners - David Charlesworth

Murder! Mystery! Mayhem!

Maggie Of My Heart – Alyson Faye
The Funeral Birds – Paula R.C. Readman
Cursed – Paul M. Feeney
The Bone Factory – Yolanda Sfetsos
Garland Cove – Deborah Sheldon
Death In The Dugout – Bruce Harris

Beats! Ballads! Blank Verse!

Book 1: Echoes From An Expired Earth – Allen
Ashley
Book 2: Grave Goods – Cardinal Cox
Book 3: From Long Ago – Paul Woodward
Book 4: Laws Of Discord – William Clunie
Book 5: Fanged Dandelion – Eric LaRocca

Weird! Wonderful! Other Worlds

Book 1: The Raven King – Liz Tuckwell
Book 2: The Wired City – Yolanda Sfetsos

Horror Novels & Novellas

House Of Wrax – Raven Dane
And Blood Did Fall – Chad A. Clark

Anthologies
The Darkest Battlefield – Tales Of WW1/Horror

WEED BY NIGHT

BY
SARAH L. JOHNSON

A SHORT SHARP SHOCKS BOOK!

BOOK 72

For further information, please visit:
WEB: www.demainpublishing.com
TWITTER: @DemainPubUk
FACEBOOK: Demain Publishing
INSTAGRAM: demainpublishing

CONTENTS

WEED BY NIGHT

It's like our first day of kindergarten, if kindergarten was a peeling grey house in the middle of bald-ass prairie. Jack and I stand in the foyer, side-by-side in our hoodies and backpacks as Mom crouches in front of us, clutching one of our hands in each of hers, squeezing tight enough to grind my knuckles. This isn't kindergarten, we're fifteen now, but I'm still scared she's not coming back.

Jack shoots me a warning scowl.

I return fire.

He rolls his eyes so slightly only I can tell he's doing it. There's a lot only I can tell about Jack. A twin thing, but Jesus Christ we couldn't be more different. We're being abandoned with strangers on a farm we didn't know existed until a few days ago. This is not normal, and how dare he pretend it is?

Behind us, a clock ticks on the fireplace mantle, and wind howls down the chimney carrying the smell of...I dunno. Old stuff, dirt, grass, and crap that makes you sneeze. I've never seen a real wood burning fireplace. Just another reminder that this isn't home, we can't go home, because we don't have one anymore.

"It's temporary." Her pretty, too-wide smile makes me nervous, like she's about to push me out a window. "It's a chance to get to know your grandparents over the summer. They're excited to have you here."

Jack and I peek over our shoulders, at the old ladies on either side of the whistling fireplace. They haven't said a word. Not one. Not even when they opened the front door to find their daughter, and the grandchildren they'd never met, on the porch. They just stared.

So excited. I raise an eyebrow.

Jack raises his. *They need to calm down.*

"I'll be back as soon as I get a place set up."

"This is bullshit," my brother mutters, wrenching his hand out of Mom's and I'm surprised as hell because that's my line. He's the good twin.

"Jack, please." Mom looks to me, eyes pleading. "Kaia?"

We've been poor before, but never this poor. Never this desperate. She doesn't want to leave us here. Jack tugs on my hood. "Just let her go."

Wind shrieks down the chimney like a wounded wolf. Mom grapples on to me, whispering through my hair. "It's time, Kaia. Girls against the world. Take care of your brother."

The same unnerving pep talk she gave me on the first day of kindergarten. All I can think is the day Jack needs *me* to take care of *him* is the day we are fully and irrevocably fucked.

Mom exchanges a wary look with the olds on either side of the fireplace, and walks out the door. Silence slams down like the lid on a stone sarcophagus. No traffic, electronics, fighting neighbors, kids playing in the park below our apartment windows, or the ever-present hum of the city. There's none of that. The clock ticks. The wind whistles. Pigeons warble. But the spaces between are deafening.

Jack makes the first move, Nikes scuffing over the floorboards. "Hi, Grandma?"

The two old women blink behind two pairs of glasses. Two plaid work shirts, two sets of cargo pants tucked into boots, and two long braids like steel bridge cables. It's impossible to tell how old they are. They seem timeless. Like they grew out of the ground exactly like this. Red shirt looks to blue shirt and nods.

Granny blue walks past us and picks up our suitcases, one in each sharp knuckled hand. Jack follows her and I follow Jack, up a staircase smelling slightly of sour carpet and groaning with every step. No sneaking around this house. The stairs end in a small landing. Grey light spills from two open doors on either side and dead ahead is another, closed.

"Attic," she says by way of explanation, somehow turning the word into a single syllable. "We're on the right, and this'll be you." She leads us into a small room with daffodil wallpaper, furnished with a desk, chair, wardrobe, and a double bed.

Jack and I exchange in a glance what would be a super involved conversation between most people. Twin brain is wicked handy in situations where it's uncool to shout WHAT THE HELL every five seconds.

Granny blue sets our suitcases in front of the wardrobe with a thump and brushes her hard hands together, looking around the room. "Get settled. Have a rest if you like, you got the run of the place. Chow time at six."

"Thanks," Jack says.

The corner of her mouth twitches. "Don't thank me yet, Jack."

"Grandma?" I call out before she can shut the door.

"Yuh?"

"Um...which..." I struggle to untangle my tongue. "Which one are you?"

Jack grimaces, like that's not an okay question to ask. But the only reason I have to ask is because everyone in this family seems allergic to the idea of proper introductions.

She peers over her glasses. "I'm your Gran, little bird."

And she's gone. Guess I know which of her mothers my mom gets her exit strategy from.

"What the shit?" I whisper the second the door clicks shut. "Omigod, this place is sketch city."

"Here we go," Jack says.

I throw my backpack on the bed and kick my shoes off in random directions, announcing my wildness in this tightly cultivated space. "Do they even have names?"

"Don't."

"Are we secretly in witness protection?"

"Now you're being dramatic."

"Have you noticed the whole house is grey? Even the G-units are the color of old newspapers."

"Color is a product of sensory processing. Maybe you have a glitch or a tumour or something."

"Or maybe it's the Twilight Zone and we're trapped some 1950s' movie about the dustbowl, or *Schindler's List*."

"The dustbowl was in the 30s, and you can't make jokes about *Schindler's List*."

"Why?"

"You just can't, so don't." He slumps into the desk chair. "They seriously expect us to sleep in the same bed?"

"Seems so," I fall on the mattress and gape at the ceiling, "because this is a horror movie. An arty one, with twincest."

"That's not even funny."

"You see me laughing?" I point at the ceiling. "Look."

"Whoa…"

My own face stares down at me from a large oval mirror mounted to the ceiling. Me, but not the me I'm used to. Gloomy light bleaches color from my hair and skin, even my eyes, like something left underwater for too long. Everything here is strange. And I don't want to look at this stranger's face anymore. "I miss—"

"Don't say it," Jack whispers, his voice hoarse, like he's trying not to cry. It makes my throat close up. A twin thing.

We shared a meat bubble for nine months. Our mom ran away from this place, smuggling us out in her belly like living contraband. She fled the prairies to raise us in the mountains. Fifteen years later, we're back on flat land.

"I was going to say I miss my phone. Do they even have a phone? I don't think they knew we were coming."

"They did look kinda surprised," Jack admits.

He's right, but the way they took us in without a word of discussion, explanation, or introduction. Like they always knew we'd come, they just didn't know when.

A grin creeps across Jack's face as he reaches into his backpack. At first I'm not sure what I'm looking at. A device, a phone, but an old one, like pre-smart.

"Mom gave it to me," he says.

"Why you and not me?"

"Probably because you'd ask too many annoying questions."

"Dick."

"She said it's for emergencies, to keep it out of sight, and that once we were here, you should hang on to it."

"She looked scared, Jack. Why would she leave us in a place she ran away from?"

"What was she supposed to do, take us to live with her in a shelter?"

I roll away from him and push my face into the pink quilt that smells like a summer storm. My mother's old bed. Whatever, I get it. Jack is the practical one, but I'm her only daughter. Girls against the world, yet she's always trusted Jack over me. He's always had more of her than I have.

The mattress dips as Jack crawls over the bed and slides the dumb-phone into my hand. I stare at the tiny black screen. "What if she doesn't come back?"

"Don't be an idiot." Jack tugs my ponytail. "We'll spend the summer here, do farm stuff, go to a meat raffle or something, and Mom'll be back in time for us to go to school."

"New school."

"I'll be your friend."

I shove his shoulder. "Shut up."

"You can even have the bed, okay?"

I almost offer to share, and it's not as fucked up as it sounds. Like a lot of broke families, we never lived anywhere big enough for us to have our own rooms, and we did share a bed until we were ten. Lots of times I miss it. The heat of him. The nearness. And that is definitely a twin thing.

***

Dinner is an experience. Jack and I watch, baffled, as Granny red opens a rectangular tin with a metal key and a cake of greased meat slides out. She slices it up and drops it sizzling into a frying pan.

Just when you think you've eaten every kind of poor kid food you can think of. "What is that?" I whisper to Jack.

Granny blue pulls a loaf of bread out of a cute wooden box on the counter. It looks homemade, the bread and the box, and I super love it. A special little home just for the bread.

"What's with the mirror on the ceiling?" I ask, cutting through the sizzle.

The Grans exchange a look I can't read through the wrinkles and Jack looks like he wants to die. Maybe it's a sex-watching thing, in which case I'm already sorry I asked, but this doesn't seem like that kind of house. And I want to know.

"It's just…strange," I add with a shrug.

Granny blue chuckles as she slides a water jug onto the table. "Your mother's old room. Only thing a proud girl loves more than being looked at, is looking at herself."

I open my mouth to argue but Jack kicks me under the table, and I want to twist his head off like a bottle cap. Why shouldn't I defend her? Why won't he? Shouldn't somebody? Why can't she be here to defend herself, and explain her weird-ass moms to us?

The SPAM is all right, at least not as gross as it looked slurching out of the can. Jack eats the way he always does when he's thinking too much to be hungry, but the bread is awesome and I demolish half the loaf myself, each slice troweled with butter. This seems to please the Grans, though I'm not sure how I know it.

Jack volunteers us for dish duty, which pisses me off because the only cool thing about crashing with strangers is not having to do chores for at least a day or two. He washes and I dry, and I don't get any credit for it because, as always, Jack is the one to make the offer.

The country has its rituals and summer evenings apparently go like this: supper, dishes, and porch sitting. Jack and I claim the front steps with their furred boards and rusty nail heads. The Grans settle into wicker chairs where one knits, and one reads what I swear to god is a dictionary. They aren't talkers. Neither is Jack. He stares down the driveway, flanked on either side by coarse mangy grass that would eat a manicured lawn for breakfast.

The wind settles and sweat collects behind my knees. I get up, brushing the splinters from the backs of my thighs, and wander around the side of the house. A path runs through the prickly grass leading to a dirt-colored building I'm guessing is a barn. Do they have animals? I tried searching up the farm on Google Earth, but all I got was pixels. Anyway, the barn gives off a serious case of the empties and I tell myself it's cooling sweat raising goosebumps on my skin.

I hurry back to the porch, finding the front steps deserted. "Where's Jack?"

The Grans merely stare as my pulse bangs in my ears. The red one smiles. I swallow, feeling the dust in my throat and between my molars. I can't be alone here. It's too lonely already.

The screen door squeals, and Jack steps out, holding up a pack of Uno cards. "Wanna play?"

Just like that. Like nothing happened. Like didn't just live an entire nightmare life of isolation in my head. Sometimes I want to kill him.

The chalky sun glides west, trailing evening shadows. Eventually Granny blue pulls out a legit old man farmer pipe and lights it. They pass the pipe between them. Smoke smelling of burnt sugar and Windex swims around their heads and spirals into the eaves of the roof overhanging the porch. I spy a bird's nest tucked into a corner. I wonder if the pigeons I heard earlier live there. I wonder if they're sleeping.

Jack and I play Uno until I get tired of losing and decide ten o'clock is a reasonable bedtime here in farmville. It's not even dark, but sleep is at least a break from the porch sitting and the weird stink of the Grans' pipe.

"Maybe they're witches," I say, wide awake on my side, avoiding even a peripheral glimpse of that damn creepy mirror. "Fattening us up for a ritual feast or some black magic pagan shit."

Jack yawns. "The way you shovelled bread in your face, you're making it easy."

"Why did Mom never talk about them?"

"Unnngh, go to sleep, Kaia."

"How can I sleep when I feel like I'm watching myself?" I roll over and blink at my dark reflection. "Something's wrong here."

The floor creaks as Jack shifts on his improvised bed. "I know."

Sleep pulls me under so smoothly I don't know it's happened until I rise into a doze, disoriented, and blind, not knowing what's disturbed me, one half of my brain fighting to put the waking half back to sleep and the waking half struggling to tell me something important before it's tugged back down into unconsciousness.

Tapping. Not loud, but insistent. Coming from the ceiling. I'm on my side, face cradled in the rain smelling pillow. The floor squeaks and Jack snuffles in his sleep as shadows race in a flickering circle on the wall across from the window. Pigeons aren't nocturnal, are they? I want to turn my head to the window but I feel my mirror-self watching with wide black eyes, smiling with all her teeth, wanting me to face her, to smile back, to expose my soft belly and warm rabbity heart, but I won't do it. She can't make me.

***

I wake up alone, swaddled in my mom's old quilt, blinking into her mirror. Do I look like her? A dumb question. My mom is pretty, like really pretty, like an expensive doll. Me, not so much. Doesn't help that a morning person, I am not, and this particular morning I'm so sleepy it's almost a physical pain. I drag myself down the stairs and shuffle into the kitchen still smelling of last night's SPAM.

Jack and Granny blue are at the table eating eggs and toast in a spray of sunshine, considerably warmer than yesterday's ashy alien glow.

"Where's the...other?" I ask.

"Won't stir for a while yet. Up late in the garden. It's her way. You take after her, I s'pose." Granny blue rinses out her coffee mug and places it on the drain board. "I'll be going into Town."

When she says Town, I think I know the one. The only place with a name in a wide radius of places identified only by geographical coordinates. A little blot of municipality, named for the pale ribbon of water running through its south end. "Milk River?"

"Said Town, didn't I?"

My cheeks flash hot. I shouldn't try to show off, but I love Google Earth. Already I miss searching up any place and zooming in on the leaves on the trees, curtains in the windows, and the cracks in the sidewalks. Not that Milk River is so special. Just another name some guy gave to something that didn't need one.

"Going to the feed store," Granny says. "Got room for one more in the truck."

"I'll go," Jack says, shocking me from walking dead to wide awake as hell.

"Why not me?" I ask.

"Too slow." He snatches my plate on his way to the sink even though I'm not done my toast.

"You have animals?" I ask Granny blue.

"Some," she replies, ambling out of the kitchen with Jack at her heel like a dumb Great Dane.

"I'll just...do the dishes," I mutter as the screen door whinges open and shut, followed a moment later by the rumble of an engine.

As I scrub egg off plates I pretend are Jack's face, I consider my strategy. The better twin. Bonding with our hosts. He's not actually better, only better at being better when there's witnesses. Not that he plans it. Jack's too good to be that devious. I dry the last plate and hold the damp towel to my face inhaling the impossible freshness of line dried linens.

Maybe he is better. Maybe the sun just shines brighter on certain people.

After the kitchen is cleaner than any kitchen I've ever cleaned before, I do a little exploring. The house isn't huge, but it's new and I like knowing the corners of places before I bounce off the walls. And I know exactly where to start.

The glass cut doorknob to the attic turns freely, but why wouldn't it? Country living means never having to lock up your shit and Granny blue said we had the run of the place. I open the door. Shadows pour down a narrow staircase, along with a darkly sweet odor drifting from the top where all I see is a slight moting of dust in the dim light. The air is different here. Swollen and humid. On the first stair, my foot seems to sink into the wood, and the railing beneath my hand feels similarly spongy. Something rustles above, causing a swirl in the dust, and my joints lock at the faint *tap, tap, tap*.

I back out and shut the door. The wind, or a rodent, or maybe the other grandmother. Whatever. The attic was closed for a reason, and I'm not a total asshole. People need their private spaces.

Doesn't take long to wander through the rest of the house, though it's way bigger than any apartment we ever had, the kind of place I always dreamed of living if we got rich. I finish where we first arrived, in the grey foyer, where I have an epiphany. One of Jack's words: epiphany. A big idea that forms in your brain super clear and perfect. It's just space. Just more rooms, and it's not like you can be in more than one at a time. The second epiphany is that houses aren't for people, so much as they are for people's stuff. Like doilies, pianos, floral sofas, knitting baskets, bookshelves jammed with encyclopaedias and old Sears catalogues, and a china cabinet full of porcelain bells, wooden frogs, and pretty bits of stone and crystal. All the junk people collect to prove they exist, so it's double weird that there's no photos of my mom. No photos of anyone.

"Creep show," I mumble, pushing through the screen door.

I step off the porch and shield my eyes against the brutal glare. The sun is different here. A gold marble in a huge blue bowl. And if I thought the house was big, it's nothing compared to the outdoors. I'm used to trees and mountains, but here the grassy horizon stretches unbroken in every damn direction, in a complete circle. Those flat earth wackadoos must have originated in the prairies. I've never seen a place so empty. So empty it presses inward, like I've found a new way to be claustrophobic.

Something wet crunches under my sneaker. I lift my foot up, look down, and scream.

"Saint Lilith save us, what in hell are you howling about?" Hard hands grab my shoulders and whip me around. I let out another hiccupping shriek as my other foot smooshes into the mess and I'm nose to nose with Granny red.

Possibly the worst idea I've ever had but I look down again. A thing, a creature, something made of meat and bone. *Bird* is the word my mind is taking too long to land on. Jack's right, I am slow. At least a dozen bloody, beaky skeletons in a crescent on the dirt. They look like lobsters. Probably related. Jesus, they stink. "Are they...pigeons?"

"Lot more where they came from," she says, grabbing a hatchet out of a steel pail on the porch, neatly chopping off the flayed little noggins, and tossing them in the pail. "Nematodes. Wee worms, live in the brain and infect anything that picks at 'em."

"What killed them?"

"Bobcat, most like."

Scavengers have already heard the carrion call. Flies coming in for a landing, ants erupting out of the dust, ready to gorge on the fanned-out corpses. "Why are they arranged like this? Is that normal?"

Granny red claps me on the shoulder. "All critters have their rituals. Come on, since you're out here, you can make yourself useful."

Squinting, I plod behind the old lady in a red shirt and overalls, wiry braid swinging back and forth, wishing to hell I had my sunglasses. She leads me down the path and behind the barn, to a garden the size of a small gymnasium, but I don't see any carrots or zucchini. Just small plants, less than a foot high, but with gently waving leaves in a distinctive seven lobe pattern. "You guys were getting high last night?"

She clears her throat. "Y'may have noticed, young lady, there are no 'guys' here."

"Right...sorry."

"This land has been in our family for generations. Our medicine is special. Makes us strong, and you won't find it growing anywhere else."

The old bird knows how to create a sense of mystery, except I'm the one eating out of her hand. I can't help it. Suddenly my mother's mothers are deeply fascinating. They have rituals and secrets. Maybe that's why we're here. Except that's not exactly true. When the thought first skips across my mind there's no we. There's just me.

"Get down here and give me a hand," she orders, not unkindly. "Damn wild grass. Can't ever keep it from creeping in."

"Invaders from planet Lawn," I say and start pulling the blades, coarser and thicker than any I've ever seen.

"Grass grows everywhere, didn't you know?" Granny red says. "Grows out of bald rock, even at the bottom of the ocean. We don't use herbicides so we got to be out here every day, otherwise it takes over. That's what happens when a plant goes to seed. Turns into a nuisance."

We pull out the encroaching blades in silence. It's peaceful down here in the jungle with the sweet clean smell of earth and chlorophyll. Not so open and empty. Almost like home. Moving along, I notice the rows aren't planted straight. They curve, around and around, in a spiral. What the hell do I know about farming? Maybe it's normal, this cornerless garden.

I don't know how long we work—the dumb-phone is tucked in my backpack upstairs—but it feels like hours. My hands sting and my legs ache from crouching but I keep going until I come across a plant much tinier than the others. "What's wrong with it?"

Granny kneels in the dirt next to me and peers at the delicate seedling, dwarfed by its neighbor. "Not a thing wrong. Taking her time is all."

I study Granny's face, brown and coarse like a baked potato. "Her?"

She gently peels a leaf back from the stalk revealing an oblong protrusion sprouting two pale pink hairs. "This here's her calyx and them little wisps are the pistils."

"She's pretty."

"More than pretty. That little bud is where her medicine comes from." She moves on to the next plant, thick-trunked tree in comparison. She tugs the leaf back from the stalk. "Now this one doesn't belong."

I take a closer look and see only a bald green pearl. "This is a male?"

"That's his pollen sac. And it only gets bigger, believe me."

"What do you do?"

"Uproot him of course, before he flowers."

"What?" My horrified tone is a surprise. It's just a plant. But calling it a 'he' makes it more. Makes him more. Makes it wrong to pull him up by his little roots when he's only barely begun to grow. "Why?"

"Same reason I cut the heads off them dead pigeons. Otherwise you'll end up with a crop gone to seed.

Males...they're like the nematodes. There's no medicine in them. All they want is to make more of themselves."

Suddenly the plant towering over the seedling no longer radiates health like a bushy green puppy. It's a hulk. A glutton. An overgrown blade of grass sucking up more than its share of sunlight. I grab it by its dumb thick stalk.

"No," Granny red wraps her hand around mine. "Uprooting under full sun can trigger a pollen release. It's a defense mechanism. Grow by day and weed by night, little bird. That's how it's done."

"I have a name."

Her rough hand squeezes mine. "So do I."

An engine growl tears through the questioning silence. Granny picks herself up and trudges off around the barn. I scamper after her like a bunny, watching her wave as Granny blue and my brother climb out of a truck that looks like it was alive during the War.

"You're a good help, Jack. If you wouldn't mind putting them sacks in the barn," Granny blue says, and arm in arm, she and Granny red disappear inside the house.

"Make yourself useful," Jack says, shoving a sack into my chest.

"Hey, I was working while you were gone." I heft the bag, barely hanging on, though I'd damn well die before admitting it. "I cleaned the kitchen...even did some gardening."

"You want a medal?"

"Asshole." I drop the sack at his feet, with extreme prejudice. It splits, spilling multicolored grains on the dirt. "I do stuff too, you know. Too bad they're always looking at you while I do it. But I wouldn't expect you to understand what it's like to be invisible, to be anything but a perfect shiny shithead." I stomp off to retrieve the wheelbarrow by the porch and feel Jack, patiently waiting for me to stop ranting like an idiot. "Don't even start with the smug. You're not better than me."

"Really? Because from where I'm standing you can't even carry a sack of birdseed. Or steer a wheelbarrow—careful!"

"Oof!" The wheel falls into a rut and I faceplant right into the bucket.

Jack pulls me up and brushes a smear of rust off my nose. "Angry driver."

I laugh. A little because it's funny. A lot because we're okay again. For now. Together we kneel in the dirt, scooping the spilled seeds back into the bag. We load the sacks into the wheelbarrow, each heft a handgrip, and trundle down the path to the barn.

"Sick," he says when we pass the garden. "That's a lotta weed."

"I don't think it's weed, exactly."

"Then what?"

"Dunno. Granny red just said it's special."

The barn door slides open and we wheel into the gloom. The smell just about smacks me to the floor. Like the smoke, but heavy and damp. Something you can sink your fingers into or stuff in your mouth and chew. Deadly sweet like a peach ripened down into a sticky puddle of itself. And something else. A hot chemical stink.

"Whoa." Jack points to row upon row of plants, huge and mature, hanging from lines strung across the barn. "These old ladies aren't playing around."

"Told you—" I scream, dropping the wheelbarrow as a loud rustling erupts above us and a warbling tsunami of beaks and beady eyes descend. The birds batter our heads with their wings and their tiny claws rake through our hair. Jack tackles me and I crash to the barn floor as the birds strafe over us and out the door. Gone as quickly as they appeared.

"Ugh, Jesus," I groan. Slimy wetness seeps through the back of my shirt, and I realize what that smell is, what I'm lying in.

"What was that?" Jack says, dusty face hovering over mine.

"Pigeons, I think."

"Guess you ought to know, being such a chicken." Jack hauls me up for the second time. "C'mon, let's get these sacks put away."

I don't give him shit for implying I'm a coward. He knows I'm not. Being startled isn't the same as being afraid.

It's not the same as being controlled by your fear and turning into blind quivering prey. Besides, I have a theory. The most dangerous thing is probably something you never think to be afraid of in the first place. That's how predators work. That's how they get you.

We leave the sacks snuggled like giant grubs against the wall. My heart is still jiffy-popping and I'm pasted in pigeon shit. Any sympathy I had for those dead feathered dickheads is down to zero. As we exit the barn, I turn to slide the door shut, peering into the fragrant gloom one last time. The dust has settled, giving me a view all the way up into the rafters, where something still rustles.

***

Supper is a feast I'm content imagining is roast pigeon and yet more bread, then it's porch sitting time. Jack and I hang out on the steps playing honest to god checkers while the G-units smoke their funky weed and read their almanacs or whatever. Already it smacks of ritual, and I don't even hate it. Doesn't stop me from complaining about how bored I am, so bored I'm jealous of all the pioneer kids in the olden days who also had no Netflix and no Google Earth, but at least had dying from diphtheria to keep things exciting.

"Shut up and make your move," Jack says, flicking away a mosquito. "Stop stalling."

I do. And he wins. Of course.

"They're robots," I suggest, bouncing onto the bed in my Bendy and the Ink Machine pajamas, and scooting under the covers. "Most advances in robotics are being made in the field of agriculture."

"Old lady farm-bots?" Jack sits on the edge of the mattress, also in his Bendy jammies, which is horrifying. We're way too old for matching anything let alone pjs. "You must miss the internet."

"Like you aren't going through porn withdrawal?"

His shoulders shudder, and he's not laughing.

"Jack, don't cry." I throw off the blankets and crawl to his side tucking my head under his chin where it fits now that he's super tall and I'm super not. "I'm sorry. I'm a dummy, a jerk, a total knob."

His skinny orangutan arms wind around me. "Kaia...I don't like it here."

"Little House on the Prairie takes some getting used to." I give him a squeeze. "But our Grandmas are kinda dope. Pot growing lesbians."

"I miss—"

"Shut up, we promised."

But I miss her too. I miss her like a chunk of meat bitten right out of my stomach. And then I have, not an epiphany, but a pretty great idea. "Let's call her. I've got the dumb-phone in my bag."

"She said only emergencies."

"How is this not an emergency?"

He shrugs. "No one is dying or hurt."

But sad is a kind of hurt and dying. Jack's pain is a bruise on my heart, and if Mom could feel it too, she'd be the one calling us. But Jack says no. So I'll do what he wants. Be what he wants. Until we stop hurting.

We crawl under the covers and fall asleep like we used to. Face to face, knees drawn up. Fetal. Connected.

A crescent moon dangles in the sky. All the bedroom furniture is gone and it smells of the barn. Burnt flowers, rotten fruit, and guano. Moonlight showers onto my long white nightgown. Little House on the Prairie style. Pretty and romantic, but if there was a fire or a tornado or something you'd be fucked because it's like wearing a five-layer straitjacket. Only place I'd ever wear this is in a dream. Therefore, I am dreaming.

Through the window a cold lunar glow falls on silver grass and a shining lady working a plot of earth with a hoe. She carves a furrow in the dirt, a single row in a perfect spiral, winding inward. At the centre, she chucks the hoe aside and reaches into the folds of her white nightie, pulling out something small and black. She drops it into the trench and sweeps soil overtop. Over and over, she seeds the earth, working her way outward along the spiral.

She looks up, sees me watching, and holds out one of the black pellets. I shouldn't be able to see from this far, or smell the blood and the rot. I shouldn't be able to hear her. But I can.

Sacred geometry, little bird.

It's not a seed or a pit in her hand, but a tiny, beaked skull.

My eyes flick open and I'm still on my side, face to face with my twin. I inhale the scent of farm laundry and the gamey aroma of teenage boy. Just a dream. Above me, a *tap, tap, tap* from the mirror. Something is trying to get my attention, and I am not afraid. I roll over and gaze up at my dark reflection. A proud girl, in a white nightie, alone in a big bed.

***

"If you're not worn out, why don't you help me bake bread this afternoon?" asks Granny blue, handing me a glass of iced tea.

I shove sweaty strands of hair off my cheeks and accept the glass, garden soil still packed under my nails, trying not to look surprised. Yesterday it seemed like Jack was her favourite and I was leftovers. "Really?"

"I'll help," the better twin says, approaching the counter.

"Women's work, Jack." She snaps a tea towel at him and tosses an apron at me. "Tie this on, little bird."

Jack flinches, eyes wide and lost. "She has a name, you know."

"Don't we all," she rejoins. "Muck out the barn if you're so keen, fill the bird feeders. Get along now."

The way he sulks off. At first it's like a cable tugging at my innards to go after him and make it all better, and maybe that's a twin thing, but I have a nagging suspicion it's a female-male thing. He can't process a reality in which he isn't picked first. No wonder he hates it here. For the first time he's living in someone's shadow. Lonely and confused. A goddamn overdue lesson and this is my epiphany: it's not my problem. Not everything is for you, Jack. Sorry if the world told you otherwise.

"Women's work?" I gulp the rest of my iced tea. "That's super sexist."

"Not if there ain't any men around," she grunts, punching down a massive bowl full of dough. "All work is our work, little bird."

"Why won't you use my name? Or tell us yours?"

"Name is a jacket people wrap 'emselves in when they figure it's their whole story. You're a bigger book than that."

"So is Jack. We're not that different. We're twins."

"I'm well aware," she says. "You should've been born in this house."

Somehow, I know she means me and not we. I haven't told Jack what I saw in the mirror. In this warm yeasty kitchen, with my grandmother bustling about, it's easy to forget the nightmares, the disturbed reflections, and the tapping. How could anything bad or scary happen here?

But that's ostrich thinking. That shit about sticking their heads in the sand is true. I wiki'd it. Ostriches are wretched beasts. Big, mean, cowards, and I am not any of those things. Especially the last thing.

I move to the sink, squirt a blob of soap in my grimy palm and start scrubbing. "Why'd my mom run away?"

Granny blue cups my chin with a flour-dusted hand, sad shadows in her eyes. "My daughter knows her mind better than I do."

"But you do know."

"And so will you, soon enough."

I can take a hint. But if she thinks sticking her head in the bread will make me go away, she's got another thing coming. We start another batch of dough in the bowl of the big stand mixer with the hook curving down like a steel root. She shows me how much flour to add and how to work the gears and clutch.

"Ow, goddamnit," I yelp as I slice my finger on a sharp edge of the housing, gritting my teeth as a drop of blood falls into the bowl. "I wrecked it."

Granny nudges me aside and starts the mixer. "Spot of blood never hurt."

The hook turns with a mechanical whir, stretching the drop of blood into a red streak against creamy dough, churning it down in a spiral. I suck on my finger, tasting steel and wheat sprouting from the dry skin of the prairies.

My blood. Baked in.

"Putting it off wouldn't change anything. She knew that." Granny stops the mixer and pulls out the dough, placing it on the counter, brushing her hands gently over the smooth, sweet mound. "We bear only daughters. If anything at all."

A lot can be said in the dark spaces between words. There's a lot of space in this house. In this family. I'm guessing Granny blue grew a baby in her belly once, but it wasn't my mom. I rest my hands on hers. Her old fingers knot with mine, pressing into the heat of rising dough.

Girls against the world.

***

"They're not so bad," I say after we've been in bed for ages, pretending to sleep.

"I didn't say they were bad," Jack snaps. "I said they don't like me."

An objection balloons in my mouth but I bite down. They don't dislike Jack. That's not it. I don't know how I know, but I do know. Intuition, I suppose. The subconscious way of knowing. Mom says I have lots of it.

"Well...I like it here," I say.

"Because they *like* you. They treat me like a stray cat, or a houseplant."

"A houseplant that does chores."

"I cleaned out that barn. There's gotta be a thousand birds in there. And there's a weird spiral design on the floor under all that pigeon shit, like a hex or a sigil."

"Sacred geometry."

His forehead scrunches. "Huh?"

He doesn't get it, and there's no way to explain how this place freaked me out at first. The horrible sun, the hugeness of the land, the wind like a wounded animal. It made me feel like a tiny little nothing. Maybe space always feels like a curse when you've been living in a cave.

"You're jealous," I say, poking him in the chest. "For once in your life you aren't the favourite."

"It's not a competition, Kaia."

"Says the loser."

"Real mature," he says, though he's the one pouting like a brat.

I glance up at the mirror, comforted by the sight of the two of us in our Bendy pjs in the double bed.

"It's just for the summer," Jack sighs and rolls away. "Enjoy it while it lasts."

Sometimes I hate him. Sometimes I imagine clobbering him with a brick. Or jamming a fork in his cheek. Sometimes I imagine him not existing at all.

I mash my face into the sharp knuckles of his spine. Punishing us both with my love. When did his shoulders get so broad? His voice so deep and bossy? When did he develop that leathery smell and why do I want to hurt him for it? The right words aren't where they usually are, and I fall asleep trying to find them.

***

Smoke wakes me up. A lot of smoke. I cough, choking on the acrid fruity stench filling the room.

"Jack," I rasp, groping around the bed, finding it empty. My reflection shows what it should. I'm in my jammies, alone in the haze. Between coughs I hear the tapping from the mirror. "Jack?"

Our door is open and my eyes sizzle in their sockets as I scramble off the bed and into the landing. I wrench the attic door open, gagging on a billow of sweet humid smoke, and launching myself up the stairs, my bare feet sticking on the damp tacky wood.

"Jack?" I shout. This is bad. Super bad. And I don't need Wikipedia or Google to tell me. It's a twin thing, screaming in my marrow, all the way down to my stem cells.

At the top I find a room with one window, exactly like our bedroom downstairs, but empty of furniture. The shadows thin as clouds clear the moon and there they are. Loose silver hair, and white nightgowns, standing over a window in the floor. The shining ladies.

Granny red holds a decapitated pigeon in her arms and its blood *tap, tap, taps* onto the glass in a gory spiral. A scream hatches in my raw throat but my feet carry me to the edge of the portal where I look down and see the messy bed I've been sleeping in the last three nights.

Granny blue beckons, ancient and beautiful in the moonglow. "It's time, little bird."

Smoke fills me like an empty jar, loosening my head off my neck, and I wonder if I'm dying.

"Our medicine," Granny red says. "It's already made you stronger. Strong enough to do what needs to be done. What your mother should have allowed you to do before you were born."

Okay, cool. Not dying. Just high as the Himalayas. There are good things about it. The panic in my throat tunnels down into my belly like a burnt animal where it has space to mellow out and feel safe again. My head expands, until it's big enough for all my thoughts and epiphanies to pull up a seat at the table, fry up some SPAM, and figure out just what the fuck is going on.

Sacred geometry.

Right above my head. Above our heads. Since before we were born. Knees up, foreheads together, germinating.

A spot of blood never hurt.

"Okay, you old bitches." My voice bangs through the smoke. "Where's my brother?"

I expect them to frown, to pucker in disapproval, the way olds do when a kid is being a vulgar little shit. But they smile. And it's terrifying.

A shock runs from the soles of my feet into my brain and I run. Down the stairs and into our bedroom, where I grab my backpack and dash out the screen door. The wind drags me up in its current, towing me off the porch and under a sky like deep black water.

I fly down the path to the barn and crash into the garden, to the centre of the spiral where I crouch, digging around in my backpack until I find the dumb-phone and thank hell it still has a charge. I dial.

"Little bird," she sighs in my ear, and my heart caves in. She's never called me that.

"Mom?"

"Are you ready?"

"Mom, I can't find Jack."

"I waited as long as I could. Longer than I should have."

I edge my way out of the garden and see a figure shambling out of the barn, a boy, roped in shadow.

"Jack!" I scream. Slowly, he turns his head in the direction of my voice. He's as stoned as I am, more even. Weaving on his feet. The smoke affects him differently. He's docile and helpless, where I'm electric and fierce. Like whatever it's giving me, it's taking from him.

"You need to be brave," Mom says. "Girls against the world, remember?"

Phone still mashed to my ear, I whip around and see the Grans in their nightgowns walking barefoot down the path. One carrying a pail, the other a hatchet.

"Mom...what's happening?"

"I took you away, Kaia." Her voice trembles. "To give you a choice. I took you away before they could choose for you."

A blade of moonlight slices across Jack's smooth cheek.

Uproot them before they flower.

"No," I whisper. "Mom, please."

She's not coming. I've got a serious situation here, and she can't bear to face it. And because my mind is so big right now, I totally get it. I too am scared enough to shit myself, but I'm no ostrich. The buzz in my bones heightens and it's not fear. It's hunger. The sun might shine on Jack but the moon glows inside of me. A pale fire. I'm where I'm supposed to be. Where I was meant to be born. My blood baked into the land.

"I love you both," Mom says, and the phone beeps dead.

It's wrong. They're wrong. I know that. Except for the first time ever I'm special. A shining lady. Mom loved Jack as much as she could for as long as she could, but he's growing up. She can't keep him, and it's my job to take him. It always was. A huge ask, if you ask me, which apparently no one is.

So, I'm left to ask myself.

They only want to make more of themselves.

There's no medicine in them.

We bear only daughters.

Sinking to my knees in the dirt, I'm still not sure. I'm too slow. A little bird with a head full of worms. Plant them all. Pull what doesn't belong. Grow by day and weed by night. That's how it's done.

I don't know if the smoke is making me feel more powerful than I am, but I focus all my brain waves into a single burst, firing it through whatever shared plasmodium exists between twins.

Don't worry Jack, I'll take care of you.

Tipping my face to the crescent moon, I close both hands around the stalk of a bushy plant towering over a seedling, and pull.

BIOGRAPHY

Sarah L. Johnson is a curly haired gladiator, maniacal runner, editor, teacher, and literary events wrangler. Her short fiction has been published in numerous anthologies and journals and she's the author of three books, Suicide Stitch: Eleven Tales (EMP Publishing), Infractus (Coffin Hop Press), and Wall of Fire (The Seventh Terrace).

She is also a co-editor at The Seventh Terrace, a Calgary-based small press for horror fiction.

ADRIAN BALDWIN (COVER ARTIST)

Adrian is a Mancunian now living and working in Wales. Back in the 1990s, he wrote for various TV shows/personalities: Smith & Jones, Clive Anderson, Brian Conley, Paul McKenna, Hale & Pace, Rory Bremner (and a few others). Wooo, get him! Since then, he has written three screenplays—one of which received generous financial backing from the Film Agency for Wales. Then along came the global recession which kicked the UK Film industry in the nuts. What a bummer! Not to be outdone, he turned to novel writing—which had always been his real dream—and, in particular, a genre he feels is often overlooked; a genre he has always been a fan of: Dark Comedy (sometimes referred to as Horror's weird cousin). *Barnacle Brat* (a dark comedy for grown-ups), his first novel won Indie Novel of the Year 2016 award; his second novel *Stanley Mccloud Must Die!* (more dark comedy for grown-ups) published in 2016 and his third: *The Snowman And The Scarecrow* (another dark comedy for grown-ups) published in 2018. Adrian Baldwin has also written and published a number of dark comedy short stories. He designs book covers too—not just for his own books but for a growing number of publishers. For more information on the award-winning author, check out:

https://adrianbaldwin.info/

DEMAIN PUBLISHING

To keep up to-date on all news DEMAIN (including future submission calls and releases) you can follow us in a number of ways:

BLOG:
www.demainpublishingblog.weebly.
com

TWITTER:
@DemainPubUk

FACEBOOK PAGE:
Demain Publishing

INSTAGRAM:
demainpublishing